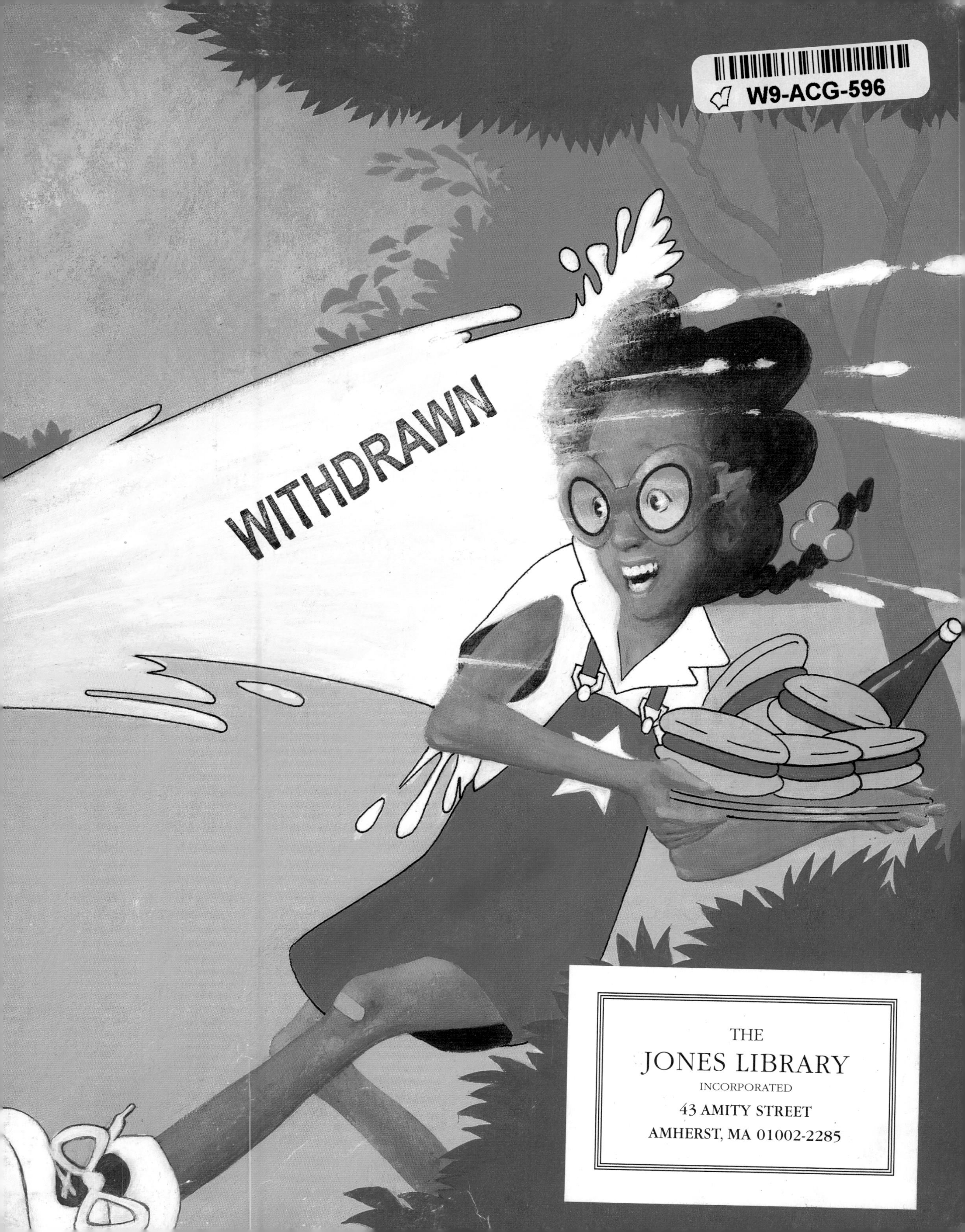

THE MOON RING

RANDY DuBURKE

chronicle books · san francisco

It was hot, hot, hot. The hottest night yet that summer.

Maxine and Grandma were trying to catch a breeze on the porch.

"Sure is hot," said Maxine.

"Mmmm," said Grandma. "And sure is some blue moon."

"What's a blue moon?" Maxine asked.

"Second full moon in a month, sweetie," said Grandma.

"Hardly ever happens. Magic loves blue-moon light."

"Where's the magic?" Maxine wanted to know.

"All around you," said Grandma. "Just feel it!"

That night, something strange
fell from the sky.
It landed in the grass,
sparkling and glowing.
Where had it come from?
What could it be?

Could it be magic?
Blue-moon magic?
Maxine decided to try it out.
"I wish . . ." she whispered,
"I wish . . . I wish . . .
I wish it was cooler!"
And suddenly . . . *WHOOSH!*

It *was* cooler!

The penguins taught Maxine how to catch fish
and the right way to walk.
Maxine taught the penguins how to dance.

A seal gave her a great ride—until...

"**YIKES!**" Maxine screamed.

"I wish I was outa here!"

And suddenly... ***WHOOSH!***

She *was*.

So were Seal and Penguin.

Penguin had never seen such unusual birds.
Seal was amazed to be so far off the ground.
Maxine loved riding with the giraffes—until ...

"**YIKES!**" screamed Maxine.

"I wish I was in New York City!"

And suddenly... ***WHOOSH!***

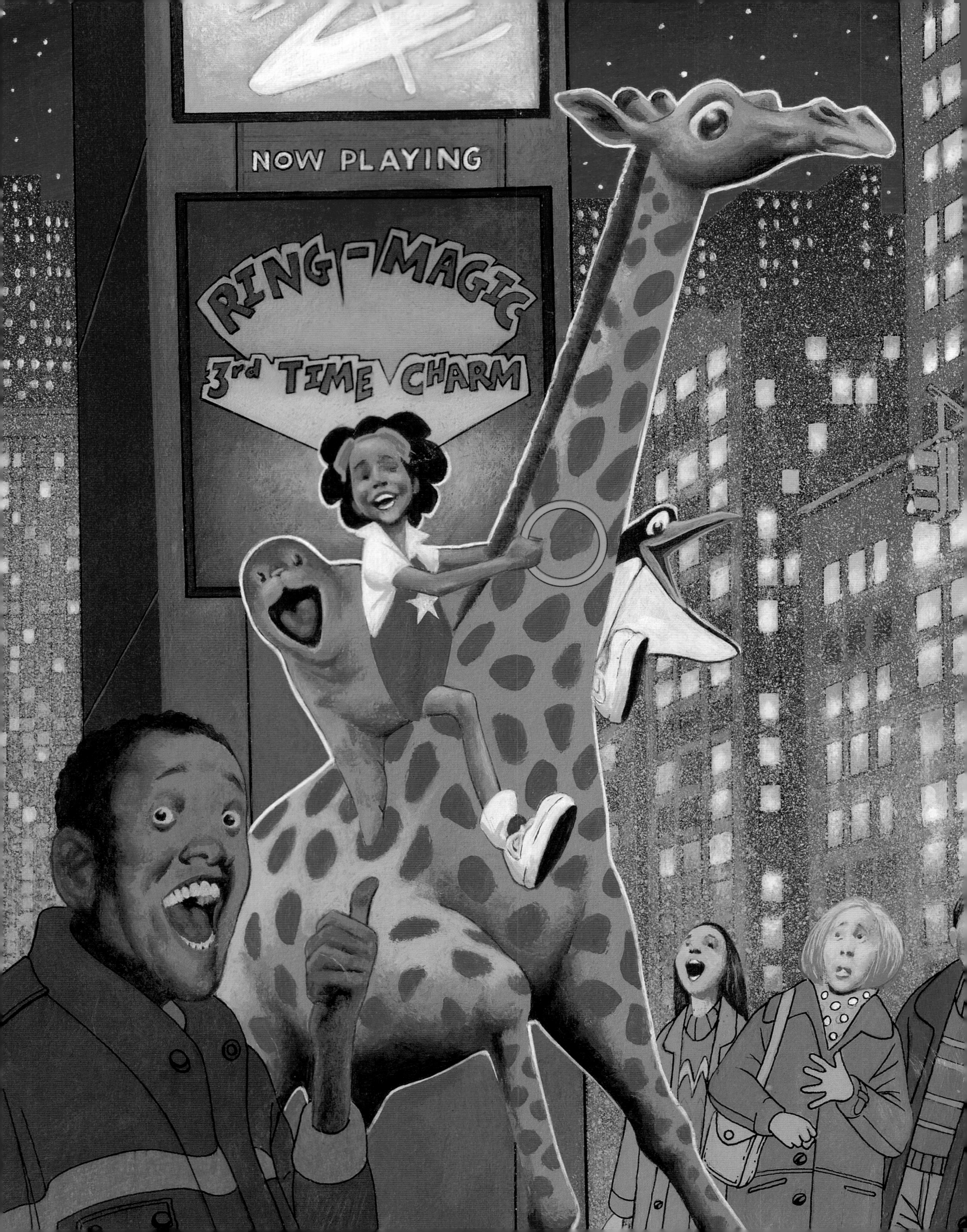
NOW PLAYING
RING-MAGIC
3rd TIME CHARM

She *was*.
So were Seal
and Penguin
and Giraffe.

Seal was astonished
by the wildlife.
Penguin marveled at the lights.
Giraffe headed straight
for the tallest thing in sight—
the Empire State Building.

The view from the top was splendid.
"I wish Grandma could see us,"
said Maxine.
And that was Maxine's fourth wish.
At that very moment,
the moon ring leapt out of her hand
and into the sky.
"Oh, no!" said Maxine.
"How will I ever get home now?"
But suddenly ... *WHOOSH!*

The moon went down,
and the sun rose up,

and Maxine was sitting
in her very own bed.

She raced to the kitchen.

"You'll never believe where I went last night!"
Maxine told her family all about her adventures.
"That sure was some dream, honey," said Ma.
"Mighty fine imagination," said Dad.
"Weird," said Louis.

But Maxine and Grandma knew better.

With love to my mother, Katie,

the inspiration for Maxine

and the model for Grandma

Special thanks to Ted, Betsy, Susan, Christy, Fred, Anna,
Tayyar, Yan, Sennur, Maija, Rickie, Evilio and Colin

Book design by Christy Hale.
Typeset in Corinthian Light.
The illustrations for this book were rendered in pen and ink and acrylic
on Fabriano 300-pound coldpress watercolor paper.
Manufactured in China.

Library of Congress Cataloging-in-Publication Data
DuBurke, Randy.
The moon ring / by Randy DuBurke. p. cm.
Summary: One hot night, Maxine goes on a wild adventure thanks to
the magic of the blue moon.
ISBN 0-8118-3487-5
[1. Moon-Fiction.] I. Title.
PZ7.D85486 Mo 2002
[E] — dc21
2001006008

Distributed in Canada by Raincoast Books
9050 Shaughnessy Street, Vancouver, British Columbia V6P 6E5

10   9   8   7   6   5   4   3   2   1

Chronicle Books LLC
85 Second Street, San Francisco, California 94105

www.chroniclekids.com